Gustave Kerker

The Belle of New York

A musical comedy in two acts

Gustave Kerker

The Belle of New York
A musical comedy in two acts

ISBN/EAN: 9783744781688

Printed in Europe, USA, Canada, Australia, Japan

Cover: Foto ©Andreas Hilbeck / pixelio.de

More available books at **www.hansebooks.com**

THE
BELLE OF NEW YORK

A Musical Comedy in Two Acts.

WORDS BY

HUGH MORTON.

MUSIC BY

GUSTAVE KERKER.

VOCAL SCORE	6s. net.
PIANOFORTE SOLO	3s. ,,
LYRICS	6d. ,,

LONDON:

HOPWOOD & CREW, Ltd., 42, New Bond Street, W

Berlin: BOTE & BOCK.

New York: T. B. HARMS & CO.

CONNICK

𝔇ramatis 𝔓ersonæ.

ICHABOD BRONSON ...(President of the Young Men's Rescue League and Anti-Cigarette Society of Cohoes)		MR. DAN DALY
HARRY BRONSON ... ... (his Son, a Young Spendthrift)		... MR. HARRY DAVENPORT
KARL VON PUMPERNICK ... ... (a Polite Lunatic)		MR. J. E. SULLIVAN
"DOC" SNIFKINS ... ... (the Father of the Queen of Comic Opera) ...		...MR. GEO. K. FORTESCUE
"BLINKY BILL" McGUIRE ... ... (a Mixed-Ale Pugilist)		MR. FRANK LAWTON
KENNETH MUGG ... ... (Low Comedian of the Cora Angelique Comic Opera Company)		... MR. GEO. A. SCHILLER
COUNT RATSI RATTATOO } (Twin Portuguese Brothers)		{ MR. WILLIAM H. SLOAN
COUNT PATSI RATTATOO }		{ MR. WILLIAM GOULD
BILLY BREEZE ... ... (a Sailor)		... MR. EDWIN W. HOFF
MR. TWIDDLES ... ... (Harry Bronson's Private Secretary)		MR. FRANK TURNER
MR. SNOOPER ... ... (a Newspaper Reporter)		MR. LIONEL LAWRENCE
MR. PEEPER ... ... (a Photographer)		... MR. D. T. MACDONALD
WILLIAM ... ... (a Butler)		MR. ALBERT WALLERSTEDT
VIOLET GRAY ... ... (a Salvation Lassie)		... MISS EDNA MAY
FIFI FRICOT ... ... (a Little Parisienne)		MISS PHYLLIS RANKIN
KISSIE FITZOARTER ... ... (a Music Hall Dancer)		MISS MABEL HOWE
CORA ANGELIQUE ... ... (the Queen of Comic Opera)		MISS HELEN DUPONT
MAMIE CLANCY ... ... (a Pell Street Girl		... MISS PAULA EDWARDES
PANSY PINNS ... ... (a Soubrette)		MISS HATTIE MOORE
BETTY "THE BAT"		... MISS MARTHA FRANKLIN
MYRTLE MINCE ...		MISS SYLVIA THORNE
QUEENIE CAKE ...		MISS ROSE WITT
BIRDIE SEED ...	(Cora's Bridesmaids)	MISS GRACE SPENCER
GLADYS GLEE ... }		{ MISS IRENE BENTLEY
DOROTHY JUNE ...		MISS EMILY SANFORD
MARJORIE MAY ...		MISS ELLA SNYDER
LITTLE MISS FLIRT		... MISS ROSE WITT
DRUMMER BOYS		{ MISS NELLY LOOMIS
		MISS DAISY THOMPSON

ACT I.—Scene 1 ... The Dining Room of Harry Bronson's House on Riverside Drive, New York

     Scene 2 ... ... The Conservatory of Harry Bronson's House

     Scene 3 ... ...Pell Street, New York, on the Chinese New Year's Eve

ACT II.—Scene 1 ... ... Smyler's Candy Store, Broadway, New York

     Scene 2 ... ... The Interior of the Grand Central Station, New York

     Scene 3 ... ...On the Lawn of the Casino at Narragansett Pier

ACT I.

THE BELLE OF NEW YORK.

MUSICAL COMEDY IN TWO ACTS.

WORDS BY
HUGH MORTON.

MUSIC BY
GUSTAVE KERKER.

Nº 1. INTRODUCTION & OPENING CHORUS—"WHEN A MAN IS TWENTY ONE."

The Belle of New York.

The Belle of New York.

TENORS.

When a man is twen-ty - one, Let him

BASSES.

When a man is twen-ty - one, Let him

drink hot rum; Let him drink it hot and cold__ When a

drink hot rum; Let him drink it hot and cold__ Hot and cold. When a

man is twen-ty-one, Let him make things hum; Let his life be free and bold, For

man is twen-ty-one, Let him make things hum; Let his life be free and bold, Free and bold, For

nev-er will you be so gay a-gain, And nev-er will you see such fun, As you

nev-er will you be so gay a-gain, And nev-er will you see such fun, See such fun, As you

will when the spark-ling cup you drain On the day when you are twen-ty-one. Then

will when the spark-ling cup you drain On the day when you are twen-ty-one. Then

The Belle of New York.

The Belle of New York.

Moderato.

guess I'm just a wee bit woo-sy, Lit-tle woo.___ Tri-fle

Lit-tle woo.___

woo.___ Could-n't blame you if you said I'm... boo sy, Lit-tle

Tri-fle woo.___

boo.___ Tri-fle boo. But I'm just a-bout to

Lit-tle boo.___ Tri-fle boo.

The Belle of New York.

take a.... bride, And I'm twen - ty - one years old be - side. Hence the

high - ness of this ri - sing tide.— Lit - tle tide.—   Ti - dy

Lit - tle tide.—

tide.—   Lit - tle

Ti - dy tide.— Oh, we guess he's just a wee bit woo - sy,

Oh, we guess he's just a wee bit woo - sy,

10

HARRY.

Lit - tle

old   be - side Hence the high - ness of his   ri - sing tide.

old   be - side Hence the high - ness of his   ri - sing tide.

tide___   Ti - dy   tide.

Lit - tle tide___   Ti - dy   tide.

Lit - tle   tide___   Ti - dy   tide.

Allegro agitato.

HOUSEMAIDS.

Oh,

naugh - ty Mis - ter Bron - son You have - n't been to bed, And in a - no - ther hour You're due, you know, to wed. The house is top - sy - tur - vy, And our dust - ing is - n't done, not done; The sweep - ing and the o - ther things Aren't e - ven yet be - gun, No not

The Belle of New York.

The Belle of New York.

16

The Belle of New York.

The Belle of New York.

HARRY.

Lit - tle

Oh, we   guess he's just a   wee   bit woo - sy,

Oh, we   guess he's just a   wee   bit woo - sy,

Nº 2. SONG & CHORUS— (CORA.) "WHEN I WAS BORN THE STARS STOOD STILL."

When I was born, the stars stood still and blink'd their eyes with wonder,
When I've been asked to be a bride, I've ne'er been known to falter,

wonder, With wonder, with wonder, And blink'd their eyes with wonder, The
falter, To falter, to falter, I've ne'er been known to falter, At the

The Belle of New York.

C.

man in the moon said,"Hul_ly gee!" And his wife said,"Well, by thun_der!" By
ten - der   age of sweet sixteen I be _ gan my trips to the al - tar. The

CORA.

thun_der!   By   thun_der!   And his wife said, "Well, by   thun_der!" For
al - tar,   The   al - tar,   I be _ gan my trips to the al _ tar! And

C.

they could see that I was a kid That was sure to make things hus _ tle, I was
ev' _ ry chance I've had since then I was migh_ty quick to   grab it, I am

Allegretto.

C.

bound to become a Pauline Hall Or a beautiful Lil_lian Russell!   And
known as the annual di _vor _ cee, And marrying is my habit.

The Belle of New York.

now I am the pet you bet of bank ers, brewers and all that set; The

i - dol of the lit - tle boys that sit up in the gal - ler-ree. When

in my diamonds I ap-pear, I look like a beau-ti-ful chan - de-lier, And

Rus-sell Sage would fall down dead If he had to pay my sal - er-ree. And

And
SOPRANO.

And
TENOR.

And
BASS.

And

The Belle of New York.

N.º 3. SONG & DANCE— (MUGG, KISSIE & BILL.) "LITTLE SISTER KISSIE."

BILL.

When lit – tle Sis – ter Kis – sie gets a
The Chap – pies nev – er lin – ger in the

jump – ing, In the flip – py, trip – py, skip – py, slip – py dance, ... You can
bar rooms, When the time ar – rives for Kis – sie to ap – pear, ... When she

bet she keeps the fid – dlers all a hump – ing, While she
starts to do her ca – pers and tar – ra – rums, You

puts the daz – zled pub – lic in a trance . . . . She has
have – n't a – ny ap – pe – tite for beer . . . . All

The Belle of New York.

made a re - pu - ta - tion with her wink - ing,   Oh, It's e -
flut - ter - ing and fun - ny does your heart feel,   It's e -

Kis - sie has the ed - u - ca - ted eye, ... She
- nough to make a par - son have a fit, ... When

sets the lit - tle Chap - pies all a blink - ing, When she
Kis - sie turns a fiz - zy, whiz - zy cart - wheel, And

turns her pret - ty slip - pers to the sky. Oh,
fol - lows up the cart - wheel with a split. Oh,

The Belle of New York.

lit-tle Sis-ter Kissie's A jaun-ty lit-tle mis-sie, She can turn a so-mer-sault or

hand-spring, Her pret-ty wink-y eye goes, She's full of dink-y - di-dos

CHORUS.

When she re-presents the art of danc-ing. Oh, lit-tle Sis-ter Kis-sie's A

jaun-ty lit-tle mis-sie, She can turn a so-mersault or hand-spring, Her

pret - ty wink - y eye goes, She's full of dink - y - di - dos

When she re - pre-sents the art of danc - ing.

ddanc - ing.

DANCE (after last verse.)

Nº 4. SONG— (FIFI.) "OH, TEACH ME HOW TO KISS."

shy   just   now,   And   I   would _ n't   know   how   To
think   that   I,   In   the   by   and   bye   At

love   like   a   thorough - bred   la _ dy;   But
kiss _ ing   might   prove   ve _ ry   han _ dy   Though

I   sur _ mise   That   I   might   grow   wise,   If   you
in _ com _ plete   I   ought to · be ·   sweet,   For you

wooed   me   in   nooks   that   are   sha _ dy —   Oh
know   that   I'm   made   out   of   can _ dy —   Oh

teach me how to kiss, dear, Teach me how to squeeze,

Teach me how to sit up_on your sym-pa-the-tic knees;

Teach me how to coo, dear, Like a tur-tle dove;

Teach me how to fon-dle you, Oh teach me how to love.........

Oh

Oh

Oh

The Belle of New York.

The Bells of New York.

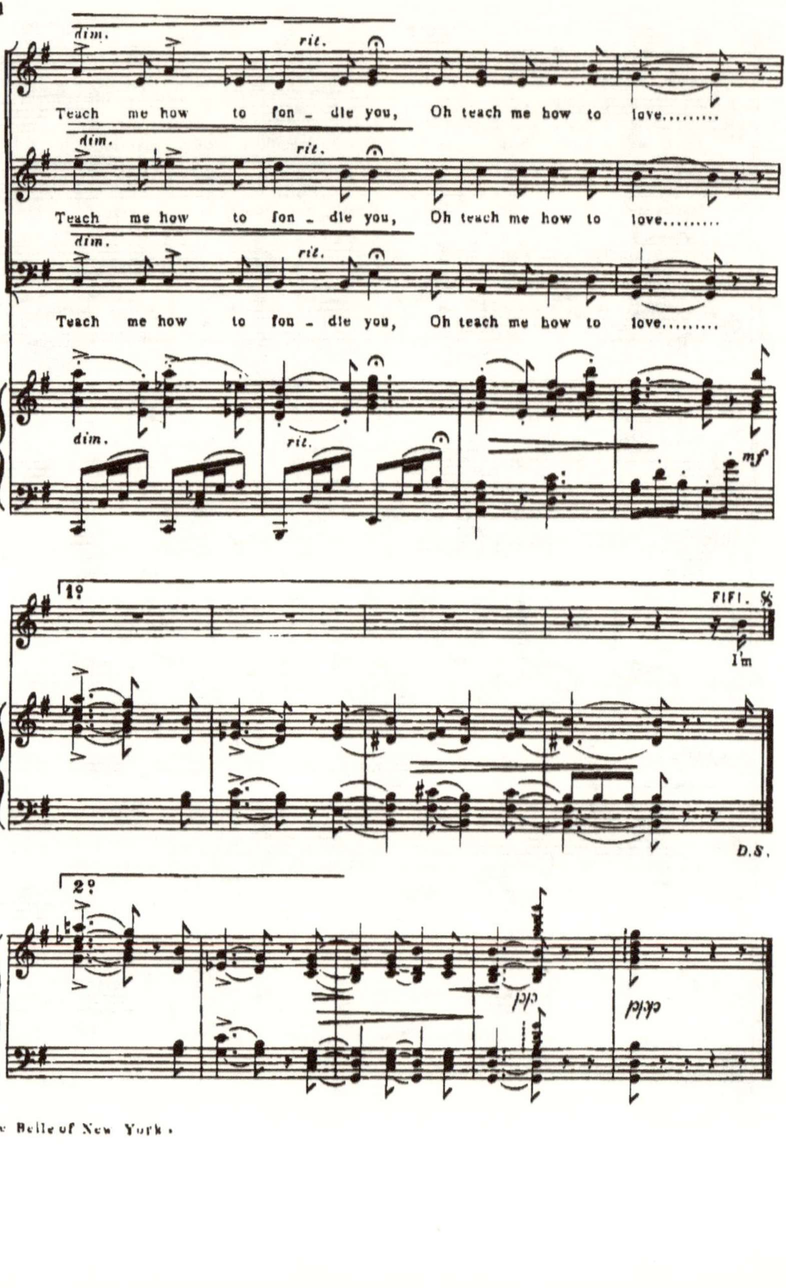
dim.
rit.
Teach me how to fon - dle you, Oh teach me how to love.........
dim.
rit.
Teach me how to fon - dle you, Oh teach me how to love.........
dim.
rit.
Teach me how to fon - dle you, Oh teach me how to love.........
dim.
rit.
mf
1º
FIFI.
I'm
D.S.
2º
ppp
ppp

N.º 5. MARCH & CHORUS — (LEAGUE & OTHERS.) "WE COME THIS WAY."

Tempo di Marcia Moderato.

PIANO.

With boom of drum,

Boom, tzing, tzing! With boom of drum,............................ And

Our souls they'll save, With

proudly flying banner. Your souls we'll save.

proud_ly fly_ing ban_ner,

Ob_serve our grave And re_ver_en_tial manner.

The Belle of New York.

Snowy plumes To their chief

he com_mand as-sumes Of the young Men's Rescue League and

An _ ti Ci _ gar _ ette So _ ci _ _ e _

ICHABOD.

From

_ ty

far   Co - hoes,   Where the   hop - vine grows,   And the
Sigh   and   weep,   With a   woe   that's   deep,   For

youth   of   the town   are   prone to dis - si - pa - tion,   This
each   of   you all   as a   mi - ser - a - ble sin - ner,   We

faith - ful   band,   Un - der   my   com - mand,   Has em -
long   and   pray   For the   bless - ed   day,   When you'd

barked   on   a tour   of   mo - ral a - gi - ta - tion,   With -
scorn   to   be seen   drink - ing   clar - et   with your din - ner,   With

_out a pause, We shall spread our cause, From the
zeal in _ tense, And at great ex _ pense, We

Hud _ son's shore to the dis _ tant Bay of Bis _ cay, The
seek to de _ stroy vi _ cious ha _ bits in our neigh bors, But

world well purge, Of the dead _ ly scourge, Of the
we re _ gret, That the ci _ gar _ ette, Gives the

cold high _ ball, And the cock _ tail made of whis _ key, For
loud Ha _ ha, To our her _ cu _ le _ an la _ bors, Yet

42

In the field of moral endeavor, No competitor can shake a stick at us, CHORUS. In the game of reform there never, no never, were reformers that were so felicitous, CHORUS. Our virtues continue to strike us, As qualities magnificent to see......... Of

stick at us

licitous

course you could never be like us, But be as like us as you're a‿ble to

be, Of course you could nev‿er be like us, But be as

like us as you're a ‿ ble to be......................

SOPRANOS.

For

TENOR.

For

BASS.

For

in the field of mo_ral en_dea_vour No com_

in the field of mo_ral en_dea_vour No com_

in the field of mo_ral en_dea_vour No com_

mf

_pe_ti_tor can shake a stick at us,.................. In the

_pe_ti_tor can shake a stick at us, stick at us. In the

_pe_ti_tor can shake a stick at us, stick at us. In the

game of re_form there nev_er, no nev_er, were re_

game of re_form there nev_er, no nev_er, were re_

game of re_form there nev_er, no nev_er, were re_

The Belle of New York.

46

The Belle of New York.

like us as you're a‿ble to be.

like us as you're a‿ble to be.

like us as you're a‿ble to be.

like us as you're a‿ble to be.

We be, 'ble to be.

be, 'ble to be.

be, 'ble to be.

be, 'ble to be.

D.S.

Allegro con spirito.

PIANO.

Where— 'er you stray The wide world through, You'll find to-day This max—im true. Who loves not wo—man, wine and song, Re—

The Belle of New York.

mains a fool his whole life long! Twas thus, that Mar _ tin

Lu _ ther sang, As Doc _ tor Mar _ tin Lu _ ther sang, Who

loves not wo _ man, wine and song, Re _ mains a fool his

whole life long................

leggiero. pp

day.......... Win _ ter's changed in _ to May.......... The

day.......... Win _ ter's changed in _ to May.......... The

day.......... Win _ ter's changed in _ to May.......... The

rit. *a tempo*

world is made bright, The heart is made light By wine, wo_men and

world is made bright, The heart is made light By wine, wo_men and

world is made bright, The heart is made light By wine, wo_men and

mf

song..... The world is made bright, The heart is made light By wine, wo_men and

song..... The world is made bright, The heart is made light By wine, wo_men and

song..... The world is made bright, The heart is made light By wine, wo_men and

ff *rall.*

The Belle of New York.

song, Hail.... All Hail, wine........ and

song, Hail.... All Hail, wine........ and

song, Hail.... All Hail, wine........ and

song..

song..

song..

Nº 8. SONG—(FIFI & BRIDESMAIDS.) "LA BELLE PARISIENNE."

The Belle of New York.

54

The Belle of New York.

which do you like ze best, M' - sieur? Now
which do you like ze best, M' - sieur? Now

which do you like to see............ Ze
which do you like to see,........... Ze

haugh . . . ty proud A - me - ri - can girl, Or ze
haugh . . . ty proud A - me - ri - can girl, Or ze

la - dy from gay Pa - ree?
la - dy from gay Pa - ree?

The Belle of New York.

BRIDESMAIDS.
CHORUS.

Oh, la belle Pa - ri - - si - - enne, She... do
belle Pa - ri - - si - - enne, She... do

cap - - ture all ze men,................. Wiz ze
cap - - ture all ze men,................. Wiz ze

naugh - - ty lit - - tle way she 'ave of
naugh - - ty lit - - tle way she 'ave of

walk - - - - ing; When a -
dan - - - cing; When a -

The Belle of New York.

The Belle of New York.

Nº 9. SONG— (ICHABOD.) "MY LITTLE BABY."

kiss you more than twice. And if you think it nice, Un . .
made a hit with me— And now if you'll a - gree— Our . .

. to those kiss . es I will add a few—...... That's what I'll
lips in os - cu - la - tion soon shall meet........ If I en -

do............ My dear to you............
. treat—.......... Will you be sweet?...........

Lay your lit - tle gold - en head on my left shoul - - der,

Darl - ing I would have you grow a tri - - fle bold - - er.

Oh, you pret - ty po - - sy, Ain't we get - ting co - - sy,

My lit - - tle ba - - by;

You're as sweet as ro - ses when they bloom on June - days,

You're as sweet as sun - light is on sum - mer noon - days,

I will nev - er lose you— I'll kiss you till I bruise you—

My lit - tle ba - by. ba - by.

62

DANCE (after last verse.)
Largamente.

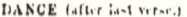

staccato.

The Belle of New York.

Nº 10. CHORUS — "PRETTY LITTLE CHINA GIRL."

The Folio of New York.

Tic-kle lit-tle Chi-na girl, Take a lit-tle yum yum, Ting-a-ling-a-ling-ling.

Tic-kle lit-tle Chi-na girl, Take a lit-tle yum yum, Ting-a-ling-a-ling-ling.

Tic-kle lit-tle Chi-na girl, Take a lit-tle yum yum, Ting-a-ling-a-ling-ling.

Lit-tle gin-ger pop, pop, Lit-tle mut-ton chop-py chop, Give her to the cop, cop,

Lit-tle gin-ger pop, pop, Lit-tle mut-ton chop-py chop, Give her to the cop, cop,

Lit-tle gin-ger pop, pop, Lit-tle mut-ton chop-py chop, Give her to the cop, cop,

Send her up to Sing Sing. Tic-kle tic-kle, tum tum, Tic-kle lit-tle Chi-na girl,

Send her up to Sing Sing. Tic-kle tic-kle, tum tum, Tic-kle lit-tle Chi-na girl,

Send her up to Sing Sing. Tic-kle tic-kle, tum tum, Tic-kle lit-tle Chi-na girl,

The Belle of New York.

(sung through the nose.)

sky . . . . high, sky . . . .
sky . . . . high, sky . . . .
sky . . . . high, sky . . . .
mf
sky . . . . high, sky . . . .

. . . . high. sky . . . . high!
. . . . high, sky . . . . high!
. . . . high. sky . . . . high!
. . . . . . high. sky . . . . high!

Aye! . . . .
Aye! . . . .
Aye! . . . .
Aye! . . . . .
ff

The Belle of New York.

Pret - ty lit - tle Chi - na gir - lie, vel - ly vel - ly nice, When she get a long way off, Ching! Ching! Take a lit - tle Chi - na gir - lie, put her on the ice, Make a lit - tle Chi - na gir - lie cough, Ching! Ching!

70

The Belle of New York.

71

Tic-kle lit-tle Chi-na girl, Take a lit-tle yum yum Ting-a-ling-a-ling.

Tic-kle lit-tle Chi-na girl, Take a lit-tle yum yum Ting-a-ling-a-ling.

Tic-kle lit-tle Chi-na girl, Take a lit-tle yum yum Ting-a-ling-a-ling.

Lit-tle gin-ger pop, pop, Lit-tle mut-ton chop-py-chop, Give her to the cop, cop,

Lit-tle gin-ger pop, pop, Lit-tle mut-ton chop-py-chop, Give her to the cop, cop,

Lit-tle gin-ger pop, pop, Lit-tle mut-ton chop-py-chop, Give her to the cop, cop,

Sing. Sing. Hi ya! Hi ya!

Sing. Sing. Hi ya! Hi ya!

Sing. Sing. Hi ya! Hi ya!

ff

The Belle of New York.

72

The Belle of New York.

The Belle of New York.

Nº 11. SONG— (VIOLET.) "THEY ALL FOLLOW ME."

The Belle of New York.

The Belle of New York.

The Belle of New York.

N⁰ 12. SONG & CHORUS — "WE'LL STAND AND DIE TOGETHER."

broth - er, now, and broth - er, It's the loy - al child and moth - er, It's the
shot and shell are fly - ing And the jol - ly boys are dy - ing, The

Stars and Stripes and Un - ion Jack to - ge - - - ther, Then
Eng - lish tars will ne - ver strike their ban - - - ner, Then

L'istesso tempo.

here's to good Old Glo - ry, And the dear old Un - ion Jack, In...

bat - tle fierce and go - ry Let's fight, boys, back to back, We won't for-get We're broth - ers yet And birds of a sin - gle fea - ther. With our flags un - furled, A - gainst all the world, We'll stand and die to - ge - ther.

CHORUS.

Then here's to good Old Glo — ry And the dear old Un - ion
Then here's to good Old Glo — ry And the dear ol Un - ion
Then here's to good Old Glo — ry And the dear old Un - ion

Jack, In... bat - tle fierce and go - ry Let's
Jack, In... bat - tle fierce and go - ry Let's
Jack, In... bat - tle fierce and go - ry Let's

fight, boys, back to back, We won't for-get We're
fight, boys, back to back, We won't for-get We're
fight, boys, back to back. We won't for-get We're

broth - ers yet And birds of a sin - gle fea - ther, With our

broth - ers yet And birds of a sin - gle fea - ther, With our

broth - ers yet And birds of a sin - gle fea - ther, With our

rit.

flags un - furled, A - gainst all the world, We'll stand and die to -

flags un - furled, A - gainst all the world, We'll stand and die to -

flags un - furled, A - gainst all the world, We'll stand and die to -

a tempo

ge - - ther.

ge - - ther.

ge - - ther.

ff

Fine.

D. C.

N? **13.** SONG— (BLINKY BILL.) "SHE IS THE BELLE OF NEW YORK."

Tempo di Valse.

PIANO.

B.B.

BLINKY BILL.

There's a great lit - tle girl in a
There is - n't a tough in a

queer lit - tle gown Who's the pride of the Sal - va - tion Ar - my,..... And
Bow - e - ry dive That is - n't dead gone on the las - sie,..... And

when she ap - pears in this part of the town; Why, she sets the whole
a - ny hot guy would - n't long be a - live If with her he should

The Belle of New York.

B.B.

neigh-bour-hood balm...y........... She's got a blue eye that's as
ev _ er get sas _ sy........... I tell you right now she's a

B.B.

bright as the sky That is smil _ ing so ten _ der a _ bove her,.....
re _ gu _ lar bird, As dain _ ty as ev _ er you saw fly;.....

B.B.

... And the boys and the girls could-n't tell you just why, But there
... And when she's a _ round, well, I give you my word Dat we

B.B.

is _ n't a one that don't love her............. Oh!
don't read a ting but de War Cry............. Oh!

The Belle of New York.

CHORUS.

She is the Belle of New York,............ The
sub - ject of all the town talk;................ She
makes the old Bow - e - ry Fra - grant and flow - e - ry,
When she goes out for a walk.............. She's

The Belle of New York.

soft as a snow-y white dove,................ She's

sim-ply cre-a-ted to love,................ The

fel-lows all sigh for her— They would all die for her—

She is the Belle of New York................

Repeat Chorus for Dance after Second Verse.

D.S.

The Belle of New York.

Nº 14. FINALE. ACT I.

Più mosso.

agitato

IC:

sir! oh, sir! I real - ly must re - fuse it. But

that would - n't be a nice thing to do.

HARRY.

I

want you to have it, if I have got to lose it. But

VIO:

I in - sist that he shall give it back to you. Oh! I've

The Belle of New York.

Moderato.

done ve-ry well up to now......... As a sim-ple lit-tle girl, As a

qui-et lit-tle girl. And I real-ly would ne-ver know how,......... To con-

-duct my-self as an heir-ess. I've lived in a mo-dest lit-tle

way,......... Like a qui-et lit-tle girl, Like a sim-ple lit-tle girl, And I

The Belle of New York.

Galop.

VIO.

If you want a mil‐lion‐air‐ess, If you're look‐ing for an heir‐ess, Here's a

lit‐tle group of la‐dies that will make your mo‐ney fly, We are

free to say we han‐ker To be chum‐my with your ban‐ker, And we'd

like to give you les‐sons in the art of roll‐ing high.

The Belle of New York.

The Belle of New York.

The Belle of New York.

The Belle of New York.

The Belle of New York.

-cept, I beg, my fa_ther's pro_po_si_tion, I shall be satis_fied if you do I will ac_cept it, sir, on one con_di_tion, That I shall re_store your wealth to you, And that will I do as quick_ly as I can, sir. For

VIOLET.

HAR:

104

The Belle of New York.

ICABOD.

Oh! she is the belle of New York,................... The

sub_ject of all the town talk..................... She makes the old

Bow_e_ry Fra_grant and flow_er_y, When she goes out for a

walk......................... She's soft as a snow_y white

The Belle of New York.

dove,................ She's sim _ ply cre _ a _ ted to love,................ The fel _ lows all sigh for her, They would all die for her, She is the belle of New York....................

Oh,

Oh,

Oh,

The Belle of New York.

110

The Belle of New York.

soft as a snow‿y white dove,.............. She's sim‿ply cre‿

soft as a snow‿y white dove,... She's sim ‿ ‿

soft as a snow‿y white dove, She's sim ‿ ‿

_ a _ ted to love................ The fel‿lows all sigh for her,

_ ply cre _ a _ ted to love.. The fel ‿ ‿ lows all

_ ply cre _ a _ ted to love The fel ‿ lows all

They would all die for her, She is the belle of New York..............

sigh for her, Oh! She is the belle of New York.

sigh for her, Oh! She is the belle of New York.

Moderato.

VIOLET.

Per _ haps it's best that I should ac _ qui _ ese............... And

VI.

thus gain time to think And save a lot of talk, If I can help this youth per _ haps he'll

VI.

bless, The mem_ry of the girl he knew as the belle of New

Very slow Waltz Tempo.

VI.

York. They call me the

VI.

belle of New York............... and a sim _ ple lit _ tle shy Sal_va_tion

The Belle of New York.

113

The Belle of New York.

116

The Belle of New York.

The Belle of New York.

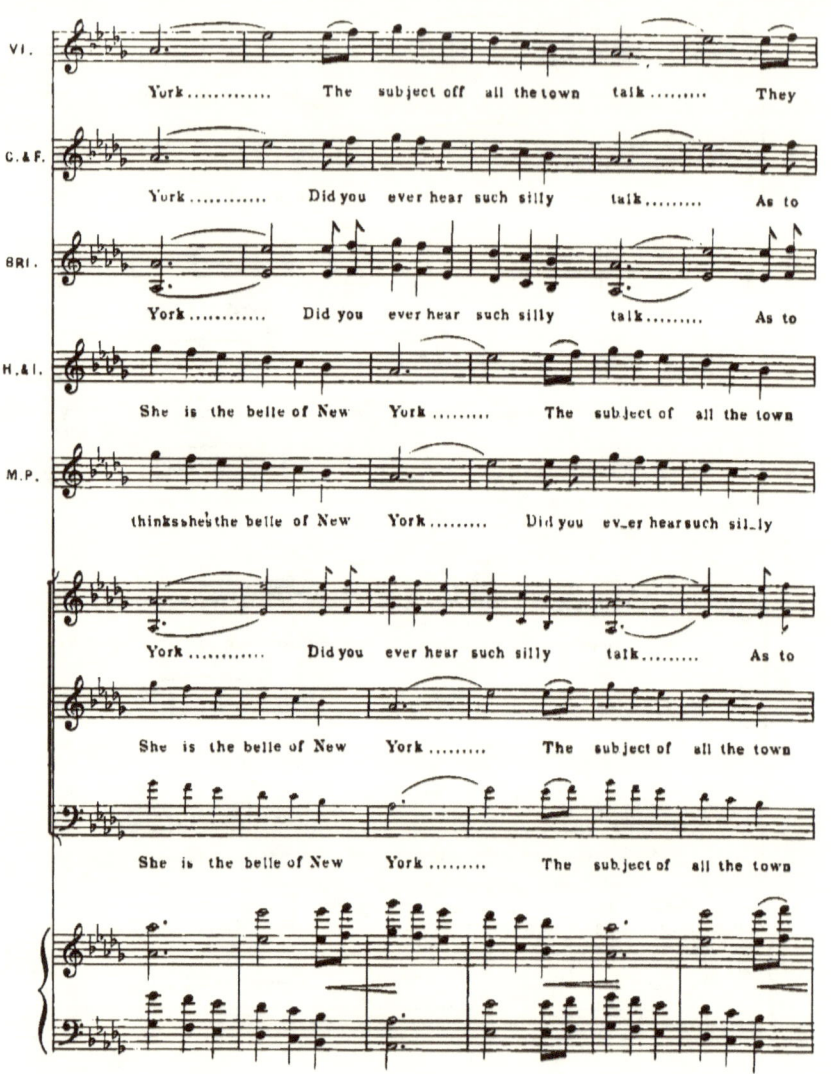

VI. York............ The subject off all the town talk......... They

C.&F. York........... Did you ever hear such silly talk......... As to

BRI. York........... Did you ever hear such silly talk......... As to

H.&I. She is the belle of New York......... The subject of all the town

M.P. thinksshesthe belle of New York......... Did you ever hear such silly

York........... Did you ever hear such silly talk......... As to

She is the belle of New York......... The subject of all the town

She is the belle of New York......... The subject of all the town

The Belle of New York.

The Belle of New York.

Tempo Imo

122

The Belle of New York.

124

The Belle of New York.

126

The Belle of New York.

The Belle of New York.

128

The Belle of New York.

VI.

talk............ Yes I am the belle of New York,............

C. & F.

talk............ She thinks she's the belle of New York,............

BRI.

talk............ She thinks she's the belle of New York,............

H. & I.

sub-ject of all the town talk............ Yes she is the belle of New York,

M.P.

sub-ject of all the town talk............ That she is the belle of New York,

talk............ Yes she is the belle of New York,............ Oh

sub-ject of all the town talk............ Yes she is the belle of New York,

sub-ject of all the town talk............ Yes she is the belle of New York,

rall.

The Belle of New York.

The Belle of New York.

132

The Belle of New York.

133

The Belle of New York.

134

The Belle of New York.

The Belle of New York.

The Belle of New York.

138

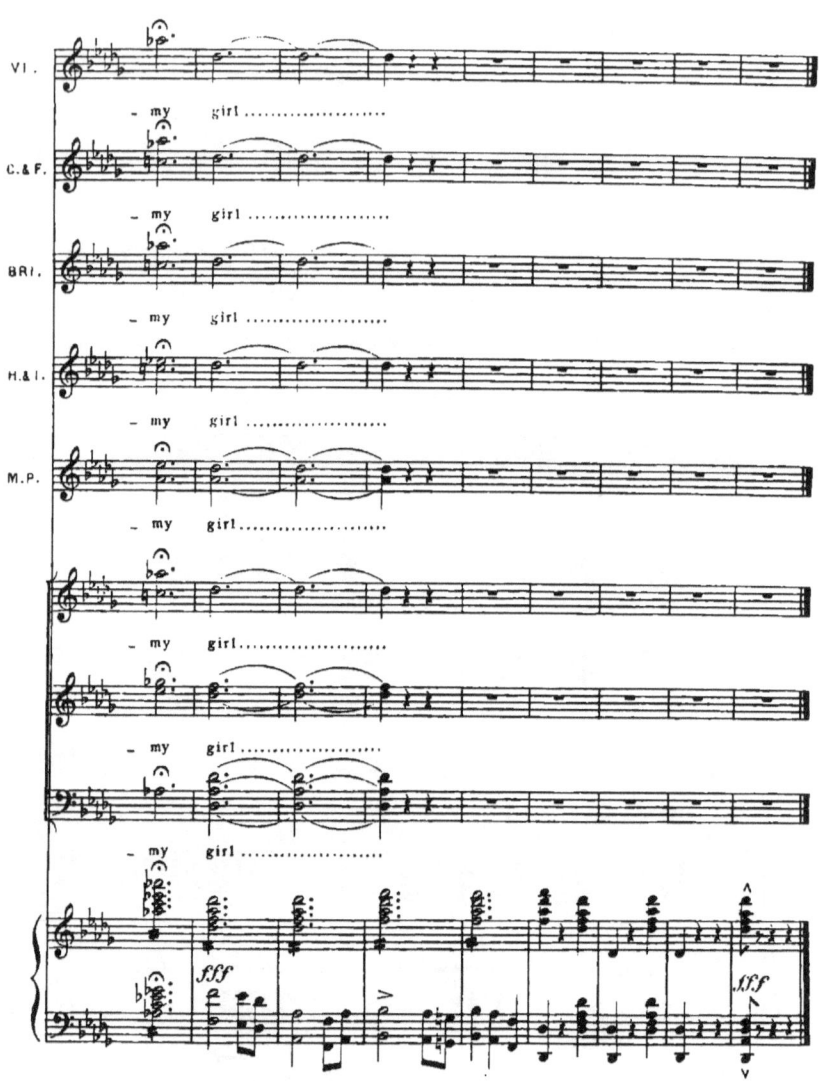

The Belle of New York.

ACT II.

Tempo di Valse.

PIANO.

The Belle of New York.

The Belle of New York.

Nº 15. OPENING CHORUS—"OH SONNY!"

Allegro agitato.

PIANO.

CHORUS.

Oh

Sonny, Sonny, Sonny, Cun't you work a lit.tle fast; Oh Son_ny, Sonny,Sonny, Don't you

leave me to the last. Oh I've got a fear_ful thirst, And I'm just a_bout to burst__ Why,

lit _ tle boy you're get_ting ve _ ry la _ _ zy. Oh

hur _ ry, hur_ry, hur_ry, And put on a lot of steam, Oh

The Belle of New York.

144

hur _ ry, hur _ ry, hur _ ry, And put in a lot of cream, Oh it's

get _ ting ve _ ry late, And I have _ n't time to wait — Now then

1°
hur _ ry up or you will drive me cra _ zy, cra _ zy, Oh

2°
HARRY.
hur _ ry up or you will drive me cra _ zy, cra _ zy, Oh

la-dies, you are rushing me to death, I have to work as hard as any

pa - vior; Just stop a bit and let me get me breath, Then

let her go a - gain and name your f's your What's your

fla - vour? What's your fla - vour? Now

let her go a - gain and name your fla - vour, Now

let her go a - gain and name your fla - vour, Now

let her go a - gain and name your fla - vour. A

glass of sars' pa - ril - la, And an - o - ther of va - nil - la, And an -

The Belle of New York.

_ o _ ther glass of o - range, and an o - ther glass of peach, Oh you

want to make 'em siz - zy, And you want to make 'em fiz - zy, And you want to serve 'em,

ALL.

son-ny, with a lot of cream in each, Oh you want to serve them, son-ny, with a

HARRY.

lot of cream in each. Oh

Moderato.

bit - ter is man's lot,   to   su - i - cide a   goa-der,   When he

works in wea-ther hot   At squirt-ing ice cream so - da;.... It's

ve - ry sad to   know........ That   I must dig and   delve it,   When

on - ly a month a - go, a - las! I   was   on   vel - vet.

girls cut loose for they have no use, For a poor lit-tle broke young

man Oh I used to roll as

high as the clouds, When I had plen-ty of mo-ney, And

I could num-ber my friends by crowds, And the world was al-ways

L'istesso tempo.

The Belle of New York.

sun _ ny, Most a _ ny girl would have been my bride, They

thought me as sweet as ho _ ney— But oh I went right

out with the tide, When I had lost my mo _ ney, But

oh I went right out with the tide, When I had lost my mo _ ney.

The Belle of New York.

been his bride They thought him as sweet as ho _ ney But

been his bride They thought him as sweet as ho _ ney But

been his bride They thought him as sweet as ho _ ney But

oh he went right out with the tide When he had lost his

oh he went right out with the tide When he had lost his

oh he went right out with the tide When he had lost his

mo _ ney, But oh he went right out with the tide When

mo _ ney, But oh he went right out with the tide When

mo _ ney, But oh he went right out with the tide When

The Belle of New York.

The Belle of New York.

The Belle of New York.

The Belle of New York.

N⁰ 16. DUET — (FIFI & HARRY.) "WHEN WE ARE MARRIED!"

The Belle of New York.

The Belle of New York.

Nº 17. ENTRANCE OF BRASS BAND.

PIANO.

The Belle of New York.

would not have you think That I would ev - er sink From
must a girl em-ploy The modes that come from Troy, Or

my high state of pi - e - ty to a - ny-thing clap-trap-py. My
is she not en - ti - tled to be stun - ning - ly New-Yorky? Oh,

mo - rals have not changed as you may guess, The
mayn't a girl be good and free from guile And

on - ly thing that's changed has been my dress, ... We're the
yet be quite a cor - ker in her style, ... We're the

The Belle of New York.

The Belle of New York.

170

The Belle of New York.

The Belle of New York.

PRINCIPALS WITH SOPRANO.

or - na - men - tal Pu - ri - ty Bri - gade, To our

pu - ri - ty we add a lit - tle fash - ion, A

pret - ty rib - bon of the pro - per shade Could

N°. 18. SONG & CHORUS – (VIOLET.) "I DO, SO THERE!"

The Belle of New York.

CHORUS.

Oh, she wants to see all the sights, She

Oh, she wants to see all the sights, She

Oh, she wants to see all the sights, She

Oh, she wants to see all the sights, She

wants to stay out at nights, She wants to see ev-'ry-thing

wants to stay out at nights, She wants to see ev-'ry-thing

wants to stay out at nights, She wants to see ev-'ry-thing

wants to stay out at nights, She wants to see ev-'ry-thing

da - ring. She wants to go ev-'ry-where tear - ing. She's

da - ring, She wants to go ev-'ry-where tear - ing. She's

da - ring, She wants to go ev-'ry-where tear - ing. She's

da - ring, She wants to go ev-'ry-where tear - ing. She's

ti - red of hum - drum things, ... She feels as though she had

ti - red of hum - drum things, ... She feels as though she had

ti - red of hum - drum things, ... She feels as though she had

ti - red of hum - drum things, ... She feels as though she had

The Belle of New York.

The Belle of New York.

The Belle of New York.

№ 19 . SONG— (BLINKY BILL.) "GOOGAN'S FANCY BALL."

Allegretto.

PIANO.

BLINKY BILL.

When I went to Mis-ter Goo-gan's Fan-cy Ball,   I was
Well, Ma-lo-ney like a gil-ly he got mad,   When I

walk-ing round the room with Dan   Ma-lo-ney,   Says
spoke a-bout the frec-kled Miss   Ma-ho-ney,   Oh, it

Dan to me, the girl that knocks 'em all   Is the
ne-ver once oc-curr'd to me she had   Come to

au - burn hair'd Le - ti - tia Ann Ma - - ho - - ney.   Says....
Mis - ter Goo - gan's par - ty with Ma - - lo - - ney.   Ma.. - -

I   to Dan   "Yer   talk - ing   through   yer   hat.   I.-
- lo - ney hit   me   once   up - on   the   jaw,   An:

- ti - - tia ain't   the   one   to   catch   the   fan - - cy.   She   is
then   I   hit   him   on   the   so - lar   ple - - xus,   The.....

ban - dy   leg - ged,   frec - kled,   and   she's   fat.   And   she
last   of   Dan   Ma - lo - ney   that   I   saw   He   was

is - - n't   in   the   game   with   Ma - mie   Clan - - cy."   Oh,
sail - ing   through   the   win - dow   bound   for   Tex - - as.   Oh,

184

The Belle of New York.

Nº 20. SONG — (ICHABOD & OTHERS.) "ON THE BEACH AT NARRAGANSETT."

Meet me on the beach, boys, down at Nar _ ra _ gan _ sett;
Life at Nar ra _ gan _ _ sett al _ ways has a fizz on,

We'll go out and have a lit _ tle swim, You'll
On the wave of plea _ sure you can glide. And

The Belle of New York.

186

find a mer – ry life, boys and girls that will en – hance it,
ev' – ry – thing you do there you put a jol – ly whizz on, And

For the Nar – ra – gan – – sett girls are full of vim. Oh, they're
you can beat the o – cean with your tide. If there's

al – ways in a state of ra – pid tran – – sit, When you
a – ny risk to take the girls will chance it When they

meet them on the beach at Nar – ra – gan – sett.
strike the gid – dy whirl of Nar – ra – gan – sett.

cresc: –

The Belle of New York.

The Belle of New York.

You'll be glad it's Sum - mer, you'll be glad that you're a - live.

You'll be glad it's Sum - mer, you'll be glad that you're a - live.

You'll be glad it's Sum - mer, you'll be glad that you're a - live.

You'll be' glad it's Sum - mer, you'll be glad that you're a - live.

D.C.

DANCE. (after second verse.)

mf

The Belle of New York.

N.° 21 . CHORUS —"FOR THE TWENTIETH TIME WE'LL DRINK."

Allegro con spirito.

PIANO.

The Belle of New York.

192

The Belle of New York.

The Belle of New York.

we've got a right to get tight to-night, If we ne-ver get tight a -

we've got a right to get tight to-night, If we ne-ver get tight a -

we've got a right to get tight to-night, If we ne-ver get tight a -

gain...... If we ne-ver get tight a - gain...............

gain......... If we ne-ver get tight a - gain.............

gain........ If we ne-ver get tight a - gain.............

a tempo

Nº 22. SONG— (VIOLET.) "AT ZE NAUGHTY FOLIES BERGERE."

men zey all smile and zey say....... Zat girl has a nice lee-tel

way........ With a tra la, la, la, la, la. la, la, la, la,

la, la, la, la, la, la, la, la, la, la, la, la, la, la, la, la, la, la,

la, la, la, la!....................... I'm

The Belle of New York.

Nº 23. FINALE — ACT II. "FOR IN THE FIELD."

-ous, Our vir - tues con - tin - ue to strike us, As qual - i - ties mag - nif - i - cent to see,...................... Of course you could ne - ver be like us, But be as like us as you're a - ble to be...........

202

The Belle of New York.

The Belle of New York.

210

END OF OPERA.

"N? 24. SONG—"YOU AND I"

Andantino.

PIANO.

When we walk up town to-geth-er on a

Sat-ur-day af-ter-noon, You and I, you and I, Oh the

day it seems de-li-cious,with our hearts in per-fect tune,You and I, you and I! When we

The Belle of New York.

212

nev - er reach the full - ness of the man up in the moon; But we
sort of own the street, And we learn to watch our feet, When we
walk up town to-geth-er, On a Sat-ur-day af - ternoon.

The Belle of New York.

When we walk up town to - geth - er on a
Sat - ur - day af - ter - noon, You and I, you and
I, Oh the on - ly thing that's sad is that the
walk should end so soon, For you and I, you and I! We....

The Belle of New York.

drop in here and drop in there, and ev' - ry drop is sweet; And there

comes a lit - tle love look in your eye, And your

fin - gers sort of cling to mine, as we go up the street, You and

I, you and I!........................ Oh of

The Belle of New York.

216

course we don't get tight, For that would-n't be po-lite! Oh, we

nev-er reach the full-ness of the man up in the moon; But the

pave-ments kind of dance, And you're in a sort of trance, When we

walk up town to-geth-er, On a Sat-ur-day af-ter-noon.

The Belle of New York.

N.º 25 . DUET — (BILLY & MAMIE.) "TAKE ME DOWN TO CONEY ISLAND ."

Allegretto.

PIANO.

BILLY.

Get   on   your pumps, mame, I'm   goin'   ter   take   yer   spiel - ing,
Treat yer   to   beer, mame, E - nough   to   float   a   steam - er,

MAMIE.

Bil - ly I'll be with you, ne - ver fear
Don't yer care, your girl has learnt to swim

BILLY.

Got ter get a move on to cure a ner - vous feel - ing
take you for a whirl, mame, that's goin' to be a screamer

MAMIE

BILLY.

ner - vous feel - ing, reach - ing o - ver here, Now
scream a - way, my Bil - ly, let her blim, I'll

B.

whis - per to your Bil - ly boy, Where d'ye want to go, Will you
take you for a don - key ride, rush yer down de chute, Oh, I'll

The Belle of New York.

Moderato assai.

Take me down to Co - ney Is - land by the sea, That's ex-act - ly what you want to do with me, take me out and boat me If you want to see me smile, Take me in - to the wa-ter and float me down at Co-ney's Isle.

The Belle of New York.

221

BILLY.

Now you're talk - in' po - try and I'll just do that.

B. Go put on your jer - sey and your new spring hat,

BOTH. Ma - mie and her Bil-ly,........ Will do the thing in style........ We'll

knock the glitter-ing pub-lic silly down to Coney's Isle...... Isle....

The Belle of New York.

Nᵒ 26. DUET. — (HARRY & VIOLET.) "MAIDEN OF GENTLE GRACE."

Valse lente. Sensuose.

HARRY. (mezzo voce.)

VOICE.

PIANO.

Maid-en of gen - tle grace,............... Be thou to me a guide,............. In the pure light of thy face,............... Vir - tue and truth a - bide;............... Lead me with pa - tient hand,...........

H. Lead me from sin a - far,................ Forth to the life that's
grand,.......... Be thou my guid - ing star,.............

VIOLET.
V. I've made con - ver - sions of this kind be - fore, They are as ea - sy as
pie,................ But real - ly I think them a ter - ri - ble bore,

HARRY.
H. How fair,................

The Belle of New York.

226

The Belle of New York.

V.

- new, At my shrine? Heart of thine, *Più presto.*

H.

Here at thy shrine This heart of mine, Lan-guish-ing

Ah..

V.

His heart lan-guish-ing droops and dies,................... He

H.

droops and dies,................ In thy be - wild - 'ring

V.

thinks in my eyes he sees Glimp-ses of Pa - ra - dise.

H.

eyes,........................ There lies my Pa - ra - dise.

The Belle of New York.

V. *mf Piu vivo.*
Sure - ly this youth pleads his cause ve - ry fer - vent - ly, Still I sus -

H. *mf*
Ah!..

V.
rall. *rit.*
- pect that he's fol - low - ing me And not "That Light".............

V. *Tempo I.*
No you must walk a - lone,

H. *pp mezzo voce.*
Maid - en of gen - tle grace,.................. Be thou to

The Belle of New York.

V. I can-not guide you a - long... the.. way, 'Tis not to me that you

H. me a guide,........... In the pure light of thy face...........

V. should a - tone For the er-rors of yes-ter-day, Mine can-not

H. .... Vir-tue and truth a - bide,.............. Lead me with

V. be..... the hand,.............. Lead-ing you o'er the bar...........

H. pa - tient hand,.............. Lead me from sin a - far,...........

230

The Belle of New York.

marcato
V.
This you must un - - der stand,.................. Faith is your
rit.
H.
Forth to the life....... that's grand,................. Be thou my
rit.
Presto.
rit.
a tempo
guid - ing star,................................ Your guid - ing star!.........
Presto.
rit.
a tempo
guid - ing star,................................ My guid - ing star!.........
Presto.
ff a tempo

N.º **27.** SONG & CHORUS. — "FATHER OF THE QUEEN OF COMIC OPERA."

The Belle of New York

father of the Queen of Co - mic Op - e - ra,........... As a

pa - rent I'm pe - cu - liar - ly u - nique,.................. And you'll ad -

- mit a fa - ther's pride and fond - ness pro - per care,......... When his

daugh - ter earns a thou - sand ev - 'ry week.................. Since her

The Belle of New York

S. in - fan - cy we hav - n't been a - part a day,........ Our af-

S. -fec - tion for each oth - er is sub - lime.......................... But a

S. mil - lion-aire has sto - len Co - ra's heart a - way,........ And I'll

S. weep a - bout it when I get the time smo - ther time, I'll

CHORUS.

S. Come a-round and weep an-oth-er time, Oh he's the

F. fa-ther of the Queen of Co-mic Op-e-ra,...... As a pa-rent he's pe-cu-li'r-ly u-

S. Quite u-nique!

F. -nique................ And you'll ad-mit a fa-ther's pride and fond-ness

F. pro-per are,.... When his daugh-ter earns a thous-and ev-'ry week......... Since her

F. in fancy they've never been a-part a day, Their af-fec-tion for each oth-er is sub-

F. -time............. But a mil-lionaire has sto - len Co-ra's heart a-way. And he'll

S. s'mother time,

F. weep a-bout it when he gets the time, s'mother time, He'll come a-gain and weep an - o - ther

F. time.

1.

2.

As

Fine.

+ Nº 28. SONG—"DON'T YOU KNOW," OR "THE LANGUID MAN."

Words by Edmund Vance Cooke.

Music by Richard Stahl.

1. This life's a hol-low bub-ble, Don't you know, A
2. It's all a hor-rid mix, Don't you know—— Business,
3. Love? You meet a pret-ty girl, Don't you know, And your

paint-ed piece of trou-ble, Don't you know; We
love, and po-li-tics, Don't you know; Clubs and
head's in such a whirl, Don't you know, That you

+ By kind permission of FRANCIS, DAY & HUNTER, London & CARL FISCHER, New York.

come on earth to cry, We grow old - er and we sigh, Old - er
par - ties, cliques and sets, Fa - shions, fol - lies, ci - ga - rettes And a
kneel down on the floor And you plead and you im - plore, And it's

still and then we die, Don't you know, We
man gets what he gets, Don't you know. Bus - 'ness?
all a beast - ly bore, Don't you know. So there's

wor - ry through each day, Don't you know, In a
that's a beast - ly trade, Don't you know, Some-thing's
real - ly no - thing in it, Don't you know, And you

The Belle of New York.

sort of, kind of way Don't you know; We are
lost and some - things made, Don't you know, And we
live just for the min-ute Don't you know, You can

hun - gry, we are fed, Some few things are done and said, We are
wor - ry and we mope, And we hang our high - est hope On the
on - ly wear one tie, Have one eye - glass in your eye One

tired, we go to bed, Don't you know.
price, per haps, of soap, Don't you know.
cof - fin when you die, Don't you know.

CHORUS.

Nº 29. SONG — + DINAH, DE MOON AM SHININ'.

(KISS ME, HONEY, DO.)

Words by Edgar Smith.

Music by John Stromberg.

1. When de cot - ton fields am with - er'd an de corn am in de
2. When my boat is on de ba - you drift - in' down de sil - ver

groun', At de ca - bin of his Di - nah dis coon's
tide, Dere's a cho-co-late col - or'd la - dy snug - glin'

al - ways hang - in' roun'; When de twi - light am all
close up by my side; With her head up - on my

ful - ed an' de sun am gone to res', Den I
shoul - der while I hold her li - ly han', Then I

se - re - nades de la - dy I loves bes'..............
hear my ba - by whis - per to her man..............

The Belle of New York.

NEW AND POPULAR SONGS.

THE LAND OF HEARTS DESIRE.

In D♭.   Sung by Miss KATE CUTLER.   D to G.

Words by
HARRY GREENBANK.

Music by
HOW'RD TALBOT.

O come, my love, and take me by the hand, And lead me

to that ever happy land, Whose sunlit skies the sweetest songs

Copyright 1896

A SPRING-TIME PARTING.

In C.   Sung by Miss STELLA GASTELLE.   D to G.

Words by
FRANK MAYHEW.

Music by
GEORGE W. BYNG.

We're parting in the spring-time, And it's one to you and me, If

sun or shadow kiss the world, If spring or autumn be. We

THE TOY MONKEY.

In E♭.   Sung by Miss LETTY LIND.   C to E.

Words by
HARRY GREENBANK.

Music by
LIONEL MONCKTON.

"Click! Click!" Said the monkey on a stick, "Never in a shop I'll

stay!" So he stroll'd around the town, Meeting Smith and Jones

Copyright 1896.

PRICE TWO SHILLINGS EACH, NET.

HOPWOOD & CREW.ʟᵗᵈ 42, NEW BOND STREET, LONDON, W.